A Christmas Carol

Charles Dickens

Adapted by Nigel Flynn

GALLERY BOOKS
An Imprint of W. H. Smith Publishers Inc.
112 Madison Avenue
New York City 10016

This book was devised and produced by
Multimedia Publications (UK) Ltd

Editor: Nigel Flynn (Acorn Press)
Designer: Janette Place
Production: Arnon Orbach

First published in the United States of America 1985 by
Gallery Books, an imprint of W. H. Smith Publishers Inc.,
112 Madison Avenue, New York, NY 10016

ISBN 0 8317 1299 6

Typeset by Waveney Typesetters, Norwich, Norfolk
Origination by DS Colour International Ltd., London
Printed in Italy by Amilcare Pizzi SpA., Milan

Contents

The Life of Charles Dickens

Charles John Huffham Dickens was born on 7 February 1812, in the English coastal town of Portsmouth, where his father, John Dickens, was a clerk in the Navy Pay Office. John Dickens was 26 when Charles was born and was an excitable, extravagant man who liked to entertain in style — a style that his meagre salary as a clerk was unable to support. This was to lead him into a succession of financial crises throughout his life.

The second of eight children, Charles was a delicate, sensitive child, unable to join in the play of other children, and he withdrew into books. Later in life, recalling his boyhood days, he wrote: "When I think of it, the picture always arises in my mind of a summer evening, the boys at play in the churchyard and I sitting on my bed, reading as if for life."

The books that he read, introduced to him by his father — books such as *Robinson Crusoe*, *The Arabian Nights*, *Don Quixote* and a child's *Tom Jones* — created for him a world of magic, wonder and adventure, a world that he himself was so vividly to create for others to enjoy in his own books.

At the age of 12 the childhood of Dickens came to a sudden and dramatic end. His father, unable to pay his large debts, was packed off to the Marshalsea Debtors' Prison in London. Within a few days the rest of the family were to join him there — all, that is, except Charles, whose education was cut short and who was made to earn his living, washing bottles, at Warren's Blacking Factory. This experience proved so shocking and humiliating to the boy that it was to haunt him for the rest of his life. "No words can express the secret agony of my soul . . . I felt my early hopes of growing up to be a learned and distinguished man crushed in my breast."

Though soon re-united with his family, the previous easy life enjoyed by Charles was never to return. Two years later, at the age of 14, his irregular and inadequate schooling ended and he began work as a clerk in a lawyer's office in Gray's Inn, London. This experience, again not a happy one, gave him two things — a lifelong loathing of the legal profession and much raw material for many of his later novels.

Dickens then became a reporter on the parliamentary newspaper *True Sun*, where his natural talent for reporting and keen observation was first recognized. He taught himself shorthand and, on the *Mirror of Parliament*, and then the *Morning Chronicle*, he was soon acknowledged as the best parliamentary reporter of the age.

In 1833, now very much the young man about town, Dickens wrote his first piece of fiction: *A Dinner at Poplar Walk*, in the *Old Monthly Magazine*. Asked by the editor to contribute more, under the pen name 'Boz', Dickens wrote a series of pieces that were collected and published in 1836 under the title *Sketches by Boz*.

The modest success of *Sketches* was followed by the enormously popular and successful *Pickwick Papers*, which was published in monthly instalments in 1836 and 1837. Pickwick became a national hero overnight, and his exploits were followed by an average of 40,000 readers. Though not yet 30, Dickens was now rich and famous.

Two days after the publication of Pickwick, Dickens married Catherine Hogarth, daughter of a fellow journalist. "So perfect a creature never breathed," he wrote of her at the time, "she had not a fault." But with time his view of her was to change, and in later years he was to admit, "She is amiable and complying but nothing on earth would make her understand me." They were to separate in 1858, when Dickens was 46.

Throughout his life Dickens enjoyed travelling. In the 1840s he journeyed to Scotland, America, France, Switzerland and Italy. And throughout this period he poured out a succession of novels that exposed the cruelty, hypocrisy and appalling poverty of early Victorian society, novels such as *Oliver Twist*, *Nicholas Nickleby*, *The Old Curiosity Shop*, *Barnaby Rudge*, *A Christmas Carol*, *Martin Chuzzlewit*, and *Dombey and Son*.

Even his novel writing (which continued to be published in monthly instalments) proved inadequate for his boundless energy and restless spirit. In the 1840s, apart from all his major novels, and work on *David Copperfield* (published in 1850), he started a daily newspaper, the *Daily News*, and a weekly magazine, *Household Words*, in addition to writing a travel book *American Notes* and a three-volume *Child's History of England*.

In all that he wrote Dickens strove to draw people together and lead them to a better understanding of each other. As he himself believed, "In this world a great deal of bitterness among us arises from an imperfect understanding of one another."

But as he grew older, the subjects he wrote of grew bleaker and the mood more grim. *Bleak House, Hard Times, Little Dorrit, A Tale of Two Cities, Great Expectations, Our Mutual Friend* and his unfinished novel, *The Mystery of Edwin Drood*, all reflect a growing pessimism.

Despite a steady decline in health, Dickens continued to give dramatic public readings of his works to packed houses in both Britain and the United States, which he visited again in 1867–68. Of these a contemporary witness reported, "He seemed to be physically transformed as he passed from one character to another; he had as many distinct voices as his books had characters; he held at command the fountains of laughter and tears . . . When he sat down it was not mere applause that followed, but a passionate outburst of love for the man."

But the strain proved too much and on 8 June 1870, during a farewell series of talks in England, he suffered a stroke, and the next day he died at his home, Gad's Hill Place, near Rochester, Kent, at the age of 58.

Two days after his death Queen Victoria wrote in her diary, "He is a very great loss. He had a large loving mind and the strongest sympathy with the poorer classes." On 14 June he was buried in Poet's Corner, Westminster Abbey, close to the monuments of Chaucer and Shakespeare.

Charles Dickens in his study at Gad's Hill Place, his home near Rochester, Kent, reproduced by kind permission of the Trustees of the Dickens House (*Dickens' Dream* by R. W. Buss)

Introduction

THE story of Scrooge and the Ghosts of Christmas Past, Christmas Present and Christmas Yet To Come, is one of the best known and loved of all Christmas stories. The idea for *A Christmas Carol* came to Dickens on 5 October 1843. On that day he took part in a great meeting in Manchester, then in the heart of industrial England, to see what could be done to help the poor. Although the meeting achieved little, Dickens decided he would write a story that would move people to do something to help those less fortunate than themselves. The story he wrote was *A Christmas Carol*.

Dickens shows us what Christmas is like for the poor and deprived, the homeless, those in need of comfort. He also shows us that it is not wealth alone that makes the spirit of Christmas. Old Ebenezer Scrooge, sitting in his counting-house, has plenty of money, but he is mean, bitter, unloved, and refuses to be touched by the spirit of Christmas. Bob Cratchit and his family, though they are poor, are happy because of one very important thing: they are kind and generous and loving to each other.

A Christmas Carol wonderfully conjures up the warmth, the excitement and the joy of Christmas. But it is also a powerful ghost story. When the ghost of Jacob Marley warns Ebenezer Scrooge that he will be visited by three spirits, Scrooge dismisses it as humbug. But they prove to be only too real and frightening. The first takes him back in time to see his past life; Scrooge is saddened and ashamed. The second shows him how others spend Christmas; Scrooge feels he is indeed a lonely and unhappy man. The third, a hooded and faceless figure, shows him what the future holds; Scrooge is terrified by the scenes he sees. At the end of the book he is a changed man, moved to tears by the innocence and gentleness of Bob Cratchit's little son, Tiny Tim.

In his desire to move his better-off readers Dickens nobly succeeded. *A Christmas Carol* sold out within days of being published. Dickens' fellow novelist William Thackeray said the book was "a national benefit and to every man and woman who reads it a personal kindness". Few who have read *A Christmas Carol* would disagree.

1 Marley's Ghost

Marley was dead. There was no doubt that Marley was dead. As dead as a doornail. Did Scrooge know he was dead? Of course he did. Scrooge and he were partners. The firm was known as Scrooge and Marley. Scrooge was Marley's only friend and the only one to attend his funeral. Not that Scrooge was at all affected by the sad event, or lost any sleep over it. But then Scrooge was a tight-fisted, grasping, scraping, clutching, covetous old sinner! And as hard and as sharp as flint.

Nobody ever stopped Scrooge in the street to say, "How are you?" No beggar ever asked him for money, or children the time of day. And no man or woman ever once, in all his life, inquired the way to such and such a place.

One cold, bleak, biting Christmas Eve, Scrooge sat busy in his counting-house. The city clocks had only just gone three, but it was already quite dark. The door of Scrooge's office was open so that he could keep an eye on Bob Cratchit, his clerk, who was copying letters. Scrooge had a very small fire, but Cratchit's fire was so very much smaller that it looked as if just one lump of coal was burning in the grate.

"A merry Christmas, uncle! God bless you!" cried a cheerful voice in the gloom. It was Scrooge's nephew, Fred.

"Bah!" said Scrooge, "Humbug!"

"Christmas a humbug, uncle! You don't mean that, surely?"

"I do. Merry Christmas! What reason have

"What else can I be when I live in such a world of fools as this? Merry Christmas! What's Christmas time to you but a time for paying bills without money; a time for finding yourself a year older, and not an hour richer? If I had my way, every idiot who goes about with 'Merry Christmas' on his lips, should be boiled in his own pudding and buried with a stake of holly through his heart. Bah!"

"Uncle!"

"Nephew! Keep Christmas your way and let me keep it in mine."

"Keep it! But you don't keep it."

"Let me leave it alone, then. Much good may it do you! Much good it has ever done you!"

"I've always thought of Christmas as a good time — a kind, forgiving, charitable, pleasant time. The only time I know of in the year when men and women open their hearts freely and think of other people as if they really were fellow-passengers to the grave, and not another race of creatures bound on other journeys. And though it has never put a scrap of gold or silver in my pocket, I believe that it *has* done me good, and will do me good. And I say, God bless it!"

you to be merry? You're poor enough."

"What reason have you to be dismal? You're rich enough."

Having no better answer Scrooge said "Bah!" again, and followed it up with "Humbug."

"Don't be cross, uncle."

At this Bob Cratchit applauded, much to Scrooge's annoyance.

"Let me hear another sound from *you*," he said, "and you'll keep Christmas by losing your job!"

"Don't be angry, uncle. Come! Dine with us tomorrow."

"Good afternoon!" growled Scrooge.

"A Merry Christmas, uncle!"

"Good afternoon!"

"And a happy New Year!"

"Good afternoon!" growled Scrooge.

His nephew left the room without an angry word, and he stopped in the outer office to wish Bob Cratchit the greetings of the season. The clerk, cold as he was, returned them cordially.

"There's another fool," muttered Scrooge, who overheard him. "With fifteen shillings a week and a wife and family and he talks about a merry Christmas!"

Letting Scrooge's nephew out, Bob Cratchit let two portly gentlemen in. Standing in Scrooge's office with books and papers in their hands, they gave a bow.

"Scrooge and Marley's, I believe," said one of the gentlemen. "Have I the pleasure of addressing Mr Scrooge or Mr Marley?"

"Mr Marley has been dead these seven years," replied Scrooge. "He died seven years ago this very night."

"No doubt his generosity lives on in his surviving partner," said the gentleman.

At the ominous word 'generosity', Scrooge frowned and shook his head.

"At this festive time of the year, Mr Scrooge," said the gentleman, "it is more than usually desirable that we should make some provision for the poor and destitute, who suffer greatly at the present time. Many thousands are in want of common necessities. Hundreds of thousands are in want of common comforts, sir."

"Are there no prisons?" asked Scrooge.

11

"Plenty of prisons," said the gentleman.

"And the workhouses?" demanded Scrooge. "Are they not still in operation?"

"They are," agreed the gentlemen, "I wish I could say they were not. They are hardly the sort of place that brings Christmas cheer to mind or body. Consequently, a few of us are trying to raise a fund to buy the poor some meat and drink and means of warmth. We chose this time because it is now that want is keenly felt and abundance rejoices. How much shall I put you down for?"

"Nothing!"

"You wish to be anonymous?"

"I wish to be left alone. I don't make merry myself at Christmas, and I can't afford to make idle people merry! Good afternoon, gentlemen!"

Seeing that it would be useless to pursue their point, the gentlemen left Scrooge to his labours.

As the afternoon progressed it grew colder and colder; piercing, searching, biting cold. In the main street a young boy, gnawed by the hungry cold as bones are gnawed by dogs, stooped down at Scrooge's keyhole to sing him a Christmas carol. But at the first sound of

"God rest ye merry gentlemen!
Let nothing you dismay!"

Scrooge seized his stick with such energy that

the singer fled in terror.

At length the hour of shutting the counting-house arrived. Scrooge got up from his desk and said to Bob Cratchit, "You'll want all tomorrow off, I suppose?"

"If convenient, sir."

"It's not convenient and it's not fair that I should pay a day's wage for no work."

Bob Cratchit smiled faintly and observed that it was only once a year.

"A poor excuse for picking a man's pocket every twenty-fifth of December! But I suppose you must have the whole day. Be here all the earlier the next morning!"

The clerk promised he would and Scrooge walked out with a growl. The office was closed in a twinkling and Bob Cratchit, with the long ends of his scarf dangling below his waist, ran home as hard as he could to play at blindman's-buff with his children.

Scrooge had his dinner in his usual, gloomy inn and having read all the newspapers, went home to bed. He lived in rooms that had once belonged to his dead partner, Jacob Marley.

They were a gloomy set of rooms, old and dreary, for nobody lived there but Scrooge.

The night was now so dark that Scrooge had to grope his way to the front door on which there was a large knocker. Having placed his key in the lock in the door, Scrooge saw in place of the knocker — Marley's face.

Marley's face! It had a dismal light about it. It wasn't angry, but looked at Scrooge as Marley used to look. And the eyes, though wide open, were perfectly motionless. That, and its livid colour, made it horrible.

As Scrooge looked fixedly at it, Marley's face disappeared and was a knocker again. Startled, Scrooge put his hand upon the key, turned it and walked in. Lighting a candle, he paused a moment before shutting the front door. He looked cautiously behind it first, as if half-expecting to be terrified with the sight of Marley. But there was nothing on the back of the door except the screws and nuts that held the knocker on. So he said "Humbug!" and closed it with a bang.

The sound resounded through the house like

thunder. But Scrooge was not a man to be frightened by echoes. He fastened the door and walked across the hall and up the stairs, slowly, holding his candle in front of him. Up Scrooge went not caring about the darkness. Darkness is cheap, and Scrooge liked it. But before he shut his own front door, he walked through his rooms to see that all was right.

Sitting-room, bedroom, lumber-room — all as they should be. Nobody under the table, nobody under the sofa, nobody under the bed; nobody in the closet; nobody in his dressing-gown hanging up in a suspicious attitude against the wall.

Quite satisfied, Scrooge closed his door and locked himself in; double-locked himself in, which was not his custom. Thus secured against surprise, he put on his dressing-gown, slippers and night cap and sat down before the fire.

It was a very low fire indeed on such a bitter night. And Scrooge had to sit, huddled up, close to it, before he could extract the least warmth from such a miserable fire. There he sat, cold and dejected until he happened to glance up. It

was with great astonishment, and with a strange, inexplicable dread, that as he looked, he saw the bell on the mantelpiece begin to swing. It swung so softly at first that it scarcely made a sound. But soon it rang out loudly, and so did every bell in the house.

Whether this lasted half a minute, or a minute, he never knew, but it seemed an hour. Then the bells ceased as they had begun, together. After the bells came a clanking noise, from deep down below, as if some person were dragging a heavy chain. It was then that Scrooge remembered that ghosts in haunted houses were often described as dragging heavy chains.

Then he heard the cellar door fly open with a booming sound, and the noise grow much louder on the floors below. Up the stairs they came. Then straight towards his door. "It's humbug still!" said Scrooge. "I don't believe it! I won't believe it!"

His colour changed though, when *it* came on through the heavy door and passed into the room before his eyes. The chain it dragged was clasped about its middle and was long and wound about

him like a tail. It was made of cash boxes, keys, padlocks, ledgers, deeds and heavy steel purses. And the body dragging the heavy chain was quite transparent.

"How now!" said Scrooge, cold as ever. "What do you want with me?"

"Much!"

"Who are you?"

"Ask me who I *was*"

"Who *were* you then?" asked Scrooge, raising his voice.

"In life I was your partner, Jacob Marley."

"Can you — can you sit down?"

"I can."

"Do it then."

The ghost sat down on the opposite side of the fireplace as if he were quite used to it. "You don't believe in me," he observed.

"I don't," said Scrooge.

"Why do you doubt the evidence of your own senses? You can see me and hear me, can't you?"

"Because they can be affected by what I've eaten. You may be a blob of mustard, a crumb of cheese, a fragment of an underdone potato —

there's more of gravy than of grave about you!"

At this the Ghost raised such a frightful cry and shook its chain with such an appalling noise that Scrooge fell down on his knees and clasped his hands before his face.

"Mercy!" he cried. "Mercy!"

"Do you believe in me or not?" asked the Ghost.

"I do. I must. But why do you walk the earth and why do you come to trouble me?"

"It is required of every man that the spirit within him should walk abroad among his fellow men and travel far and wide. If that spirit does not go forth in life, it is condemned to do so after death. It is doomed to wander through the world and see what it might have shared in life."

Again the Ghost raised a cry, and shook its chain and wrung its shadowy hands.

"You are bound in chains," said Scrooge, trembling. "Tell me why."

"I wear the chain I forged in life. I made it link by link and yard by yard. My spirit never went beyond our counting-house. I spared no time for charity. Or my fellow men."

Scrooge trembled more and more. "Jacob," he said imploringly. "Old Jacob Marley, tell me more. Speak comfort to me, Jacob."

"I have none to give. For seven years I have travelled, with no rest, no peace. My only companion has been remorse — remorse for the lost opportunities."

The Ghost held up its chain at arm's length and flung it heavily upon the floor. At this Scrooge began to quake exceedingly.

"Hear me!" cried the Ghost. "My time is nearly gone. I am here tonight to warn you that you have a chance and hope of escaping my fate."

"You were always a good friend to me, Jacob, thank'ee!"

"You will be haunted by Three Spirits."

"Is that the chance and hope you mentioned, Jacob?" demanded Scrooge in a faltering voice.

"It is."

"I — I think I'd rather not."

"Without their visits," said the Ghost, "you cannot hope to escape my fate. Expect the first when the bell tolls one."

"Couldn't I take 'em all at once, and have it over, Jacob?"

"You will see me no more. But you will remember what I said."

When it had said these words the Ghost walked backwards from Scrooge and at every

step it took, the window raised itself a little, so that when the Ghost reached it, it was wide open. It beckoned Scrooge to approach, which he did. Marley's ghost held up his hand and Scrooge stopped not so much in obedience, as in fear.

From outside the window he could hear a dreadful sound of wailing and moaning. He could see the air filled with phantoms, every one of them wearing chains like Marley's ghost. Many had been known to Scrooge personally in their lives.

Closing the window, Scrooge examined the door by which the Ghost had entered. It was double-locked, as he had locked it with his own hands, and the bolts were undisturbed. He tried to say "Humbug!" but stopped at the first syllable. And feeling much in need of rest, due to the lateness of the hour, his glimpse into the spirit world and the conversation with a ghost, he went straight to bed and fell asleep upon the instant.

2 The Ghost of Christmas Past

When Scrooge awoke, it was still dark. He scrambled out of bed and groped his way to the window. He had to rub the frost off with the sleeve of his dressing-gown before he could see anything, and he could see very little even then. All he could make out was that it was very foggy and extremely cold.

He went back to bed. "Was it a dream or not?" The thought went over and over in his mind, but he could make nothing of it. Then he remembered, suddenly, that the ghost had warned him that he would receive another visitor at one. Scrooge lay in bed, waiting for the church clock to strike the hour. It was so long in coming that more than once he was convinced that he must have dozed off and missed it. At length it broke.

"Ding, dong!"
"A quarter past," said Scrooge, counting.
"Ding, dong!"
"Half past!"
"Ding, dong!"
"A quarter to!"
"Ding, dong!"
"The hour itself," said Scrooge triumphantly, "and nothing else!"

He spoke before the bell sounded, which it now did with a deep, dull, hollow, melancholy *ONE*. Light flashed up in the room and the curtains of his bed were drawn aside by a hand. Starting up, Scrooge found himself face to face with a strange figure — like that of a child.

The face had not a wrinkle on it. The arms were long and muscular; its legs, delicately

formed, were bare. It wore a tunic of the purest white and round its waist was bound a belt with a beautiful glow. But the strangest thing about it was that it was shrouded in a clear, bright jet of light.

"Are you the spirit, sir, whose coming was foretold to me?" asked Scrooge.

"I am." The voice was soft and gentle.

"Who and what are you?" demanded Scrooge.

"I am the Ghost of Christmas Past."

"Long past?"

"No. Your past."

Scrooge then made bold to inquire what business brought him there.

"Your welfare," said the Ghost.

Scrooge thanked him for his concern.

The Spirit put out its strong hand and clasped Scrooge gently by the arm. "Rise and walk with me."

Pleading that the hour was late and the weather far too cold for walking, and that anyway he had a bad cold and was wearing just his nightgown, slippers and nightcap, gently, but firmly, the Spirit led him to the window.

"But I'm only human," cried Scrooge. "I might fall and hurt myself if we go out the window."

"Bear but a touch of my hand *there*," said the Ghost, laying it on his heart, "and you shall be upheld!"

As the words were spoken, they passed through the wall and stood on an open country road, with fields on either side. The city had entirely vanished. The darkness and the mist had vanished with it, for it was a clear, cold, winter day, with snow on the ground.

"Good heavens!" said Scrooge, clapping his hands together. "I was bred in this place. I was a boy here!"

The Ghost looked at him mildly. "Your lip is trembling. And what is that on your cheek?"

"A pimple, nothing more. Now, take me where you must."

"You remember the way?" asked the Spirit.

to him — what good had it ever done him?

After the last of the boys had gone past Scrooge and the Ghost left the road, and soon they came to a dull, red-brick building. The walls were damp and mossy now, the windows broken, the gates decayed, and the outbuildings were overgrown with long grass.

"The school is not quite deserted," said the Ghost. "A solitary child, neglected by his friends, is left there still." Scrooge said he knew it, and he began to sob.

They went, the Ghost and Scrooge, to a door at the back of the school. It opened onto a long, bare room, made barer still by rows of empty wooden desks and chairs. At one of these a lonely boy sat reading. Scrooge sat down upon a chair and wept to see his poor forgotten self as he had used to be. His sobs grew louder, drowning the sound of the mice scurrying under the floorboards and the swinging of an old, half-broken door.

The Ghost touched his arm and pointed to his younger self. Suddenly a man in foreign clothes, wonderfully real and distinct to look at, stood outside the window, holding a donkey by a lead.

"Why, it's Ali Baba!" exclaimed Scrooge. "One Christmas he came to visit, when I was left all alone!"

And drying his eyes, he muttered, "I wish — but it's too late now."

"Remember it! I could walk it blindfold."

They walked along the road, Scrooge recognizing every gate and post and tree, until a little market-town appeared in the distance, with its bridge and church and winding river. A group of schoolboys came down the street in high spirits, shouting and laughing.

As the merry band approached, Scrooge knew them and named them, every one. But why was he so happy to see them? Why did his cold eye glisten and his heart leap? What was Christmas

"What's the matter?"

"Nothing," said Scrooge. "Nothing. There was a boy singing a Christmas carol at my door last night. I should like to have given him something, that's all."

The Ghost smiled thoughtfully, and waved its hand. "Let's see another Christmas!"

Scrooge's former self grew larger at these words and the room became a little darker and more dirty. The wood panels shrunk, the windows cracked; plaster fell out of the ceiling. Scrooge's former self was again alone.

He was not reading now, but pacing up and down. Scrooge looked at the Ghost and with a shaking of his head, glanced anxiously towards the door. It opened and a little girl, much younger than the boy, came darting in, and putting her arms round his neck and kissing him, said, "I've come to bring you home, dear brother."

"Home, little Fan?" replied the boy.

"Yes, yes. Home for good. Home for ever and ever! Father's so much kinder then he used to be, that home's like heaven. He said you should come home and sent me in a coach to bring you. We'll be together all Christmas long and have the merriest time in all the world."

"You're quite a woman, little Fran."

"Always a delicate creature, your sister," said the Ghost. "But she had a large heart!"

"So she had," cried Scrooge. "You're right."

"She died a woman and had, as I think, children."

"One child," said Scrooge.

"Ah yes. Your nephew, Fred!"

Scrooge seemed uneasy in his mind, and answered briefly, "Yes."

Although they had but that moment left the school behind them, they were now in the busy streets of a city. By the noise and the bustle and the shop windows, it was plain that it was Christmas. It was evening and the streets were lit.

The Ghost stopped at a warehouse door and asked Scrooge if he knew it.

"Know it! I was apprenticed here."

They went in. At the sight of an old gentleman in a wig, sitting behind a high desk, Scrooge cried in great excitement, "Why, its old Fezziwig! Bless his heart, it's Fezziwig alive again!"

Old Fezziwig laid down his pen and looked up at the clock, which pointed to seven o'clock. He rubbed his hands, adjusted his waistcoat and laughed all over. Then in a rich, fat, jovial voice he called out, "Yo ho, there! Ebenezer! Dick!"

Scrooge's former self, now a grown young man, came briskly in, accompanied by his fellow apprentice.

"Dick Wilkins, to be sure!" said Scrooge to the Spirit. "Bless me. There he is. Poor Dick! He was very much attached to me, was Dick. Poor Dick! Dear, dear!"

"Well boys," said Fezziwig, "no more work tonight. It's Christmas Eve. It's time to put the shutters up. Clear away, my lads, and let's have lots of room here!"

There was nothing they would not have cleared away or could not have cleared away, with old Fezziwig looking on. It was done in a minute. Then the floor was swept and washed, the lamps trimmed and lit, and fuel heaped on the fire. The warehouse was soon snug and warm and dry, and as bright a ballroom as you could wish to see on a cold winter's night.

In came a fiddler with a music-book, and began to play a jolly tune. In came Mrs Fezziwig, a beaming smile on her big round face. In came her three daughters and their friends; in came all the young men and women employed in the business; in came the housemaid with her cousin the baker; in came the cook with her brother's best friend, the milkman. In they all came, some shyly, some boldly, some gracefully, some awkwardly, some pushing, some pulling; in they all came until it

seemed as if all the town was there. And then off they all went, dancing round and round the room and up and down the middle, for what seemed hours, until the poor fiddler was quite exhausted and in need of a rest.

"Well done!" cried out Mr Fezziwig, clapping his hands and laughing, while the fiddler plunged his face into a pot of ale brought to him by Mrs Fezziwig, herself. And there were cakes and pies and puddings and salads, great rounds of beef and turkey, all washed down with plenty of wine and beer.

Then, taking Mrs Fezziwig by the arm, old Fezziwig stood up to dance, and off they all went again, dancing round and round the room and up and down the middle. There were more dances after that, and some games of forfeit and blindman's-buff, then yet more dances. It was not until the clock struck the hour of eleven o'clock that the party began to break up.

Only after wishing each and every guest a "Merry Christmas" did young Ebenezer and Dick leave for their humble beds under a counter at the back of the shop.

It was not until now, when the bright lights had died down, that Scrooge remembered the Spirit of Christmas Past and became conscious of his looking at him closely.

"It's a small thing, to make these silly people so full of gratitude," said the Ghost.

"Small!" replied Scrooge, indignantly.

"Fezziwig spent but a few pounds on this party. Is that so much that he deserves such praise?"

"It isn't the money he spent on the party that counts," retorted Scrooge. "The happiness he gives is as much as if he had spent a fortune."

He felt the Ghost glance at him, and stopped.

"What's the matter," asked the Ghost.

"Nothing particular," said Scrooge.

"Something, I think?" the Ghost insisted.

"No," said Scrooge. "No. I should like to be able to say a word or two to my clerk Bob Cratchit just now! That's all."

Scrooge and the Ghost again stood side by side in the open air.

"My time grows short," said the Ghost. "We must be quick!"

This produced an immediate effect, for Scrooge again saw his former self. He was older now, a man in the prime of life and his face had begun to show signs of care and greed. There was an eager, restless look about him, that had not been there before.

He was not alone, but sat by the side of a pretty young girl in whose eyes there were tears.

"It matters little," she said softly. "To you very little. Another idol has displaced me."

"What idol?"

"A golden one."

"You mean money? There's nothing wrong in making money. And nothing harder in the world than poverty."

"You fear the world too much," the girl answered, gently. "All your other hopes have been forgotten. I have seen all your good intentions fall away, one by one, until one passion, that of gain, consumes you."

"I am not changed towards you," replied Scrooge. But the girl shook her head and said, "Our love is an old one, born when we were both poor and content to be so — until, in good time, we could improve our fortune by hard work, together. You *are* changed; you are a different man now."

"I was a boy," retorted Scrooge, impatiently.

"Your own feeling tells you that you are not what you were. Those things that promised happiness when we were one in heart are now beset with misery."

"Have I ever sought release from you?"

"In words, no. Never."

"In what, then?"

"In a changed nature, an altered spirit. Tell me, Ebenezer, truthfully, if you had never loved me, would you try to win me now? If you were free now you would only have a place in your heart for a rich girl — then you really would be gaining something for yourself: you, who judge everything in life by wealth and gain."

Before Scrooge had time to reply, the girl continued. "This may cause you some pain now, but in a very short time you will think of me, when I have gone, as an unprofitable dream. Goodbye, Ebenezer, may you be happy in the life you have chosen."

Again, Scrooge began to say something, but the girl was gone.

"Ghost!" said Scrooge, "show me no more! Take me home. Why do you delight in torturing me?"

"One shadow more!"

"No more!" pleaded Scrooge. "No more. I don't wish to see it. Show me no more!"

25

But the Ghost held Scrooge in both his arms and forced him to see what happened next.

They floated unseen over snow-covered rooftops, between smoking chimneys, until they came to another scene and place: a room, not very large or handsome, but full of comfort. Near to the fire sat a beautiful young girl, so like the last girl that Scrooge believed it was the same, until he saw *her*, now much older, sitting opposite her daughter.

The two laughed heartily. There were other children too, laughing and playing in the cosy room. A knock on the door was heard, and a man laden with Christmas toys and presents entered the room to be met with shouts of wonder and delight.

The children scaled him, with chairs for ladders, some hugging him, some trying to rob him of his parcels. Their shouting and their struggling and sound of wild delight filled all the house. But soon, too soon, the children and their emotions left the parlour and, one slow stair at a time, climbed to their rooms, where they went to bed.

Now Scrooge looked on more closely than ever when the master of the house, with his daughter leaning fondly on him, sat down with her and her mother by the fireside. And when Scrooge thought that such another creature, just as pretty and graceful as she, might have called *him* father, his eyes grew very dim indeed.

Shortly, the man turned to his wife with a smile. "Belle, I saw an old friend of yours this afternoon."

"Who was it?"

"Guess!"

"How can I? I don't know." Then she added in the same breath, laughing, "Mr Scrooge."

"Mr Scrooge it was. I passed his office window, and there he was, all alone. His partner is dying, I hear. He's quite alone in the world, now, I do believe."

"Ghost!" said Scrooge in a broken voice. "Remove me from this place."

"I told you these were shadows of the things that have been. They are not of my making."

"Leave me! Take me back. Haunt me no longer!"

Scrooge suddenly felt exhausted, overcome by drowsiness. Looking round, to his surprise, he was suddenly back in his own bedroom. Barely had he time to reel into his bed, before he sank into a heavy sleep.

3 The Ghost of Christmas Present

In the middle of a prodigiously tough snore, Scrooge awoke. Again he heard the bell strike one o'clock again. But, though no shape appeared, he was struck by a violent fit of trembling. Five minutes, ten minutes, a quarter of an hour went by, yet nothing came. All this time, however, he lay in bed bathed in a blaze of light which had streamed upon him as soon as the clock had struck one.

After a while he began to think that the source and secret of this ghostly light might be in the room next door. So, getting up, he shuffled in his slippers to the next door.

It *was* his room. There was no doubt about that. But it had undergone an amazing transformation. The walls and the ceiling were hung with holly, mistletoe and ivy, and the fire gave such a mighty blaze as it had never known in Scrooge's time. Heaped up on the floor were turkeys, geese, game, poultry, great joints of meat, sausages, mince pies, plum puddings, red-hot chestnuts, apples, oranges, pears and huge Christmas cakes.

And presiding over the whole scene sat a jolly giant, glorious to see, holding a glowing torch up high. "Come in, come in!" he said on seeing Scrooge peeping round the door.

"I am the Ghost of Christmas Present! You've never seen the like of me before!"

"Never," answered Scrooge.

"Perhaps you've met my older brothers?"

"I don't think I have," said Scrooge. "Have you many brothers?"

"More than eighteen hundred."

"A large family to provide for!" muttered Scrooge.

The Ghost of Christmas Present rose.

"Take me where you wish," said Scrooge.

"Touch my robe!"

Scrooge did as he was told, and held it fast. In an instant all the contents of the room vanished. So did the fire, the hour of night and the room itself. They stood in the city streets on Christmas morning. Snow lay thickly on the ground. The sky was gloomy and there was nothing very cheerful in the climate or the place. Yet there was an air of cheerfulness abroad that the clearest summer air and the brightest summer sun would have envied.

The people who were shovelling away the snow from paths and streets were full of glee, many of them now and again throwing a snowball in good-natured fun. Some of the shops were still open, selling bread and meat and

fish and fruit and nuts and sweets to last-minute purchasers. Everyone seemed to be in a hurry, yet always stopping to exchange greetings with friends and neighbours.

Soon the steeples called good people all to church and chapel. Then from side streets and turnings came a crowd of poorly-dressed people carrying their dinners to the bakers for cooking. The sight of these poor people seemed to interest the Ghost very much. Standing with Scrooge in the baker's doorway, he took off the covers of the dinners as they passed by and sprinkled incense on them from his torch.

"Is there a special flavour in what you sprinkle from your torch?" asked Scrooge.

"There is. My own."

"Would it apply to any kind of dinner on this day?"

"To any kindly given. To a poor one most."

"Why to a poor one most?"

"Because it needs it most."

It was a very uncommon sort of torch, for once or twice when there were angry words between some dinner-carriers who had pushed each

29

other, the Ghost shed a few drops of water on them from his torch and their good humour was restored. For they said it was a shame to quarrel on Christmas Day. And so it was!

Together, Scrooge and the Ghost went on, invisibly, as they had been before, into the suburbs of the city.

There they went straight to Bob Cratchit's house. On the threshold of the door, the Ghost smiled and blessed the house with a sprinkling of his torch.

Peering inside they saw Mrs Cratchit with her daughter Belinda laying the table for Christmas dinner, while young Peter Cratchit plunged a fork into a saucepan of potatoes. Then two smaller Cratchits, a boy and a girl, came tearing in, asking when their dinner would be ready.

"Well, I don't know what's happened to your father and Tiny Tim," said Mrs Cratchit. "And where's your sister Martha?"

"Here's Martha, mother!" cried the two young Cratchits.

"Why, bless your heart, my dear, how late you are!" said Mrs. Cratchit, kissing her.

"We had to work late last night and clear up this morning, mother!" said Martha.

"Well sit down before the fire and have a warm, my dear."

"No, no! There's father," cried the two young Cratchits. "Hide Martha, hide!"

So Martha hid herself when she saw her father coming with Tiny Tim on his shoulders.

"Where's Martha?" he asked, looking around.

"She's not coming," said Mrs Cratchit.

"Not coming on Christmas Day?"

Seeing her father so disappointed, even if only for a joke, was more than Martha could bear, so she came out from behind the door and ran into his arms.

"And how did Tiny Tim behave in church?" asked Mrs Cratchit.

"As good as gold," said Bob, "and even better. Somehow he gets thoughtful sitting by himself so much, and thinks the strangest things you ever heard. He told me, coming home, that he hoped the people saw him in church because he was a cripple. Then they could remember on Christmas Day who made lame beggars walk and blind men see."

As Bob said this, Tiny Tim's little crutch was heard tap-tapping on the floor and, escorted by his brother and sister, in came Tiny Tim to make his way to his stool before the fire.

When dinner was done and the cloth was cleared, the room swept and the fire made up, the whole Cratchit family gathered round the hearth. Apples and oranges were put on the table and a shovel-full of chestnuts on the fire.

"A Merry Christmas to us all, my dears," said Bob Cratchit. "God bless us!"

"God bless us every one!" said Tiny Tim, who sat very close to his father's side on his little stool. Bob held the boy's withered little hand in his, as if he loved the child and wished to keep him by his side and dreaded that he might be taken from him.

"Spirit," said Scrooge, "tell me if Tiny Tim will live."

"I see a vacant seat in the poor chimney corner," replied the Ghost, "and a crutch without an owner, carefully preserved. If these shadows remain unaltered by the future, the child will die."

"No, no," said Scrooge. "Oh no, kind Spirit! Say that he will be spared."

"If those shadows stay unchanged by the future, then he will die," said the Ghost. "But what of that? That will simply rid the population of one who cannot help himself."

Scrooge hung his head in shame.

"Will you decide who shall live and who shall die," continued the Ghost. "It may be that in the sight of Heaven you are less fit to live than thousands like this poor man's helpless child."

Trembling, Scrooge cast his eyes to the ground. But he raised them again on hearing his own name.

"Mr Scrooge!" said Bob, raising his glass and proposing a toast. "I give you Mr Scrooge, the founder of the feast."

"I wish I had him here," cried Mrs Cratchit, "I'd give him a piece of my mind to feast upon."

"My dear, the children; Christmas Day."

"Even on Christmas Day I'm sure he's the same odious, stingy, hard, unfeeling man as he is all the year round. Nobody knows it better than you do, poor fellow."

"My dear," Bob replied, "it's Christmas Day."

"I'll drink his health for your sake and the Day's," said Mrs Cratchit, "not for his. Long life to him! A merry Christmas and a Happy New Year! He'll be very merry and very happy I've no doubt!"

The children drank the toast after her, but with no pleasure. Scrooge was the ogre of the family and the mention of his name cast a dark shadow on the party which was not dispelled for five minutes. Then the chestnuts and the fruit were passed round and round and when all was jolly and warm again, Tiny Tim sang a song in a plaintive little voice, and sang it very well indeed.

The Cratchit's were not a handsome family. They were not well dressed. Their shoes were worn and their clothes were frayed. But they were happy, grateful, and they all loved one another.

Outside, it was getting dark and snowing pretty heavily. And as Scrooge and the Spirit passed along the streets, the brightness of the roaring fires in kitchens, parlours and all sorts of rooms was wonderful. The flickering of fires showed signs of cosy dinners being prepared and deep red curtains, ready to be drawn, to shut out the cold and darkness. Everywhere children were running out into the snow to meet their sisters, brothers, cousins, aunts, uncles, and to be the first to greet them. From the number of people in the streets you would have thought that no one was at home to give them welcome when they got there.

Then, without a word of warning from the Ghost, Scrooge found himself mysteriously transported to a bleak and desolate moor, where there were great stones scattered about, like some graveyard of giants. Frost covered the ground and the only thing that grew was moss and coarse grass. In the west the setting sun had left a streak of fiery red, but now this vanished in the thick gloom of darkest night.

"What place is this?" asked Scrooge.

"A place where miners live, who labour in the bowels of the earth. But they know me. See!"

A light shone from the window of a hut and swiftly they advanced towards it. Passing through the wall of mud and stone they found a cheerful crowd assembled round a glowing fire. The Spirit did not stay here, but beckoned Scrooge to hold his robe and passing on above the moor, sped on, on, and out to sea.

To Scrooge's horror, looking back, he saw the last of the land, a range of rocks, behind them. His ears were deafened by the thundering of water as it roared and raged against the cliffs. There, built on a dismal reef of rocks some distance from the shore, stood a lonely lighthouse. Great heaps of seaweed clung to its base, and storm-birds rose and fell around it, screeching in the cold night air.

Even here, the two men who looked after the light had made a special fire and, joining their coarse hands over the rough table where they sat, wished each other a merry Christmas, and toasted each other with rum and beer, and struck up a seafaring song.

Then on sped the Ghost again, his bewildered

prisoner beside him, and all Scrooge could hear now in the blackness was the great moan of the wind about his ears. It was a great surprise to him, then, to suddenly hear a hearty laugh; and it was a much greater surprise to recognize it on second hearing as his own nephew's, and to find himself in a bright, gleaming room, with the Spirit smiling by his side and looking at the same nephew with a warm smile.

"Ha, ha!" laughed Scrooge's nephew. "Ha, ha, ha! He said that Christmas was a humbug. He believed it too! Ha, ha!"

"More's the shame for him, Fred!" said Scrooge's niece.

"He's a comical old fellow really," continued Scrooge's nephew, "and that's the truth. His wealth is no use to him. He doesn't do any good with it. He doesn't even make himself comfortable with it."

"I've no patience with him," said Scrooge's niece, and all the ladies agreed with her.

"Oh, I have!" cried Scrooge's nephew. "I'm sorry for him. I couldn't be angry with him if I tried. After all, who suffers most from his sick whims? Himself, always. Still, when he takes it into his head to dislike us, and not come and dine with us on Christmas Day, what's the difference? He doesn't miss out on much of a meal —"

"I think he loses out on a very good meal indeed!" interrupted Scrooge's niece, and again all the other ladies agreed with her.

"Well, I'm very glad to hear it," replied Scrooge's nephew, and he revelled in another laugh.

"Do go on, Fred," said Scrooge's niece, clapping her hands. "He never finishes what he begins to say! He really is such a ridiculous fellow!"

"I was only going to say that in not joining us and making merry he is missing some pleasant moments, which could do him no harm. I mean to give him the same chance every year, whether he likes it or not, for I pity him. He can't help thinking better of it if he finds me going there, year after year, in good temper, and asking him. And I think I shook him yesterday."

Then they all laughed at the notion of Fred shaking Scrooge, and the conversation ended for tea, after which there was singing round the piano. But they didn't devote the whole evening to music. After a while they played a game of forfeits, for it is good to be children sometimes — and never better than at Christmas, when its founder was a child himself.

Then followed a game called 'Yes and No'. This involved Scrooge's nephew thinking of something and the rest of the party trying to find out what by asking him questions to which he could answer just 'Yes or No', as the case might be.

From the brisk fire of questions it was soon discovered that the subject was a rather disagreeable animal that sometimes grunted and growled and sometimes talked and lived in London and walked about the streets. At every fresh question put to him, Fred burst into a gale of laughter. At last one of the guests, a plump lady, cried out, "I know what it is, Fred! I'm sure I know what it is!"

"What is it?" cried Fred.

"It's your uncle Scr-o-o-o-oge!"

"You're right, you're right, it is!" cried Fred. "But since he's given us so much merriment, it would be ungrateful not to drink his health. Here's a glass of mulled wine, everyone. To 'Uncle Scrooge!'"

"Uncle Scrooge!" they all cried.

"A Merry Christmas and a Happy New Year to the old man, wherever he is."

Uncle Scrooge was so affected by this that he would have replied had not the Spirit whisked him off again on their travels. Much they saw and far they went and many homes they visited,

but always with a happy end.

It was a long night — if it were only a night, for Scrooge had lost all sense of time. At length, the Spirit said, "My life upon this globe is very brief. It ends tonight."

"Tonight!" cried Scrooge.

"Tonight at midnight. The time is drawing near."

The bells were ringing three quarters past eleven at that moment.

"Forgive me asking," said Scrooge suddenly, "but I see something strange huddled by your side."

They were a boy and a girl. Wretched, ragged, hideous, miserable, they clung to the Ghost of Christmas Present.

Scrooge started back, appalled. "Spirit, are they yours?"

"No they are Man's. The boy is Ignorance. The girl is Want."

"Have they no home? cried Scrooge.

"Are there no prisons?" asked the Spirit, imitating Scrooge. "Are there no workhouses?"

The clock struck twelve.

Scrooge looked about him for the Ghost. As the last stroke of midnight ceased, he remembered old Jacob Marley, and lifting up his eyes, saw a solemn Phantom, draped and hooded, coming, like a mist along the ground, towards him.

4 The Ghost of Christmas Yet To Come

The Phantom approached slowly, silently. When it came near him, Scrooge fell down on his knees. The Phantom was shrouded in a deep black garment, which concealed its head, its face, its form, and left nothing visible but an outstretched hand.

"Am I in the presence of the Ghost of Christmas Yet To Come?" asked Scrooge.

The Spirit neither spoke nor moved.

"You are about to show me shadows of the things that have not happened, but will happen. Is that so, Spirit?"

"Ghost of the future! I fear you more than any spectre I have seen. But as I know your purpose is to do me good, and as I hope to live to be a better man than I was, I will follow you. But will you not speak to me?"

The Ghost gave no reply. The hand was pointed straight before them.

"Lead on, Spirit! Lead on!"

The Phantom moved away. Scrooge followed and seemed to be carried along in the shadow of the Phantom's garment. In an instant the city sprung up all around them and the Spirit stopped beside a little group of men. Seeing that the hand pointed to them, Scrooge stepped forward to listen to their talk.

"No," said a fat man with a huge chin, "I don't know much about it. I only know he's dead."

"When did he die?" asked another.

"Last night, I believe."

"Why, what was the matter with him? I thought he'd never die."

"God knows," said the first man, with a yawn.

Again the Spirit did not speak, but the upper part of the garment moved as if it had nodded its head. Although Scrooge was by now well used to ghostly company, he feared the silent shape so much that his legs trembled beneath him.

"What's he done with his money?"

"Well, I know he hasn't left it to *me*. That's all I know."

At this, the little group laughed.

"It's likely to be a very cheap funeral anyway," said a man with a red face, "for upon my life I don't know of anybody to go to it."

"I don't mind going if a lunch is provided," added a man with a pointed chin. Again the group gave a laugh, and then broke up.

Scrooge knew the men well and looked towards the Spirit for an explanation, because, for the life of him, he didn't know what they were talking about.

The Spirit glided on down the street. Its finger pointing to two persons meeting. They were men of business, too. Very wealthy and of great importance. Scrooge knew these men, also, very well.

"How are you?" said one.

"How are *you?*" returned the other.

"Well, the Devil has got his own at last, hey?"

"So I hear," returned the second. "Cold, isn't it?"

"Seasonable for Christmas, though. Good morning!"

Not another word was said. That was their meeting, their conversation and their parting.

Scrooge was surprised that the Spirit should attach importance to conversations apparently so trivial. But feeling that they must have some hidden purpose, he considered what it could be. Scarcely about the death of Jacob, his old partner, for that was past and this Ghost was concerned with the future. Nor could Scrooge think of anyone to whom he could apply what he had heard.

Quiet and dark, beside him stood the Phantom with its outstretched hand. They left the busy street and went into an obscure part of the city where Scrooge had never been before. The streets were foul and narrow, the shops and houses wretched, the people ugly and poor. The whole area reeked with crime, filth and misery.

In the heart of this district there was a tumble-down, rat-infested pawnshop, where iron, old rags, bottles and junk of all kind was brought. Inside the shop, the floor was littered with heaps of rusty keys, nails, chains, hinges, files, scales and weights. And sitting among the wares he dealt in was an old man, calmly smoke a pipe.

As Scrooge and Phantom appeared, unseen, a woman came bustling into the shop, carrying a heavy bundle. But she had scarcely entered when another woman, also carrying a large bundle, came in too. And she was closely followed by a man dressed in black, and looking remarkably like an undertaker, who was no less startled to see the two women than they were at seeing each other.

After looking at each other in astonishment for a few moments, all three burst out laughing.

"You couldn't have met in a better place," said old Joe, the man who kept the shop. "Come into the parlour. Just let me shut the door of the shop, then come on into the parlour!"

The two women followed as they were bid. On entering, the first woman, whom Scrooge recognized as his old charwoman, threw her bundle on the floor and said, "What odds, Mrs Dilber? Every person has a right to take care of themselves. I know *he* always did!"

"That's true indeed!" said Mrs Dilber. "No man more so."

"Very well, then! Who's the worse for the loss of a few things like these? Not a dead man, I suppose?"

"No indeed," said Mrs Dilber, laughing.

"If he wanted to keep them after he was dead, why wasn't he natural in his lifetime? If he had been, he'd have had somebody to look after him when he was struck by death, instead of lying gasping, alone by himself."

"It's the truest word that was ever spoke,"

said Mrs Dilber. "It's a judgment on him."

"Come on," said Old Joe, "open your bundle, let's see what you've got."

But instead of the charwoman opening her bundle first, the man in black produced his plunder. It was not extensive: a seal, a pencil-case, a pair of buttons and a brooch of no great value. These were examined by Old Joe, who chalked up the sums he agreed to pay for each item on the wall, adding them up into a total when there was nothing more to come.

"That's your account," said Joe, "and I wouldn't give another sixpence, if I was to be boiled for not doing it. Who's next."

Mrs Dilber was next. Sheets and towels, two silver teaspoons and a few boots. Her account was stated on the wall in the same manner.

"I always give too much to the ladies," said Old Joe. "It's a weakness of mine."

"Now undo my bundle, Joe," said the charwoman.

"What do you call this? Bed-curtains!"

"That's what they are."

"You don't mean to say that you took 'em down, rings and all, with him lying there."

"Yes I do. Why not?"

"You were born to make your fortune, and you'll certainly do it. What else yer got?"

"This shirt what would have been wasted if it hadn't been for me."

"What do you call wasting of it?" asked Old Joe.

"Putting it on him to be buried in," replied the woman with a laugh. "Somebody was fool enough to do it, but I took it off again."

Scrooge listened to this in horror. Old Joe, producing a flannel bag with money in it, proceeded to pay each of his three customers in turn.

"This is the end of it," said the charwoman at

last. "He frightened everyone away from him when he was alive, to profit us when he was dead. Ha, ha, ha!"

"Spirit," said Scrooge, shuddering from head to foot. "I see, I see. The case of this unhappy man might be my own. My life tends that way, now, I know. But I have seen the error of my ways. Merciful heaven, what is this?"

He recoiled in terror, for the scene had changed and now he almost touched a bed. A bare, uncurtained bed, on which there lay a something beneath a sheet. The room was dark, too dark to see clearly. A pale light fell straight on the bed and on it lay the body of a man.

He lay alone in the dark, empty house. A cat was scratching at the door, and there was the sound of rats beneath the fireplace. Scrooge glanced towards the Phantom. Its steady hand was pointing to the head of the dead man lying on the bed. Scrooge longed to draw aside the sheet to see whose body it was. But he had no more power to do so than to dismiss the ghostly

Phantom at his side.

"Spirit," he said, "this is a fearful place. In leaving it, I shall not leave its lesson, trust me. Let me go!"

Still the Ghost pointed with an unmoved finger at the head.

"I understand you," said Scrooge, "and I would if I could. But I have not the power, Spirit. I have not the power."

Again the Ghost seemed to look on him.

"If there is any person who is affected by this man's death, show me that person, Spirit, I beg you."

The Phantom spread its dark robe before him for a moment, like a wing, then, withdrawing it, revealed a room in daylight, where a mother and her children were.

She was expecting someone, for she walked up and down the room, looking out of the window and glancing at the clock. At length the long-expected knock was heard. She hurried to the door and met her husband, who sat down to the dinner that his wife had kept for him by the fire. When she asked him what news he had to tell, he seemed reluctant at first to answer.

"Is it good or bad?" she asked.

"There is hope yet," he replied.

"If *he* relents there is. Nothing is past hope, if such a miracle has happened."

"He is past relenting, he's dead."

She was a mild and loving creature by nature. But when she heard her husband's news she clapped her hands for joy and said, "Then we may sleep tonight with light hearts!"

Yes, their hearts were lighter and it was indeed a happier house for this man's death. When Scrooge heard that *he* had been a merciless moneylender, his face froze.

"Oh let me see some tenderness connected with this man's death," he cried. But the Phantom only led Scrooge silently through a maze of narrow streets until they came to Bob Cratchit's house.

Mrs Cratchit was sitting, sewing by the fire with her children. All except Tiny Tim. Laying down her work on the table, Mrs Cratchit put her hand up to her face and said in a weary voice, "My eyes grow weak by candle-light. Your father's late."

"I think he's walking a little slower than he used to the last few evenings," said Peter.

"I have known him walk with — I have known him walk with Tiny Tim on his shoulder, very fast indeed."

"And so have I, mother," cried Peter. "Often."

"He was very light to carry," continued Mrs Cratchit, "and his father loved him so, that it was no trouble — no trouble. And there is your father at the door!"

She hurried out to meet him. Bob was very cheerful with them and spoke pleasantly to all the family. "I wish you could have gone, my dear," he said to his wife, after a while. "It would have done you good to see how green a place it is. But you'll see it often. I promised Tiny Tim that I would walk there on a Sunday. My little child! My little, little child!"

He broke down all at once. He couldn't help it. The two young Cratchits got up on their father's knees and laid, each child, a little cheek against his face, as if to say, "Don't mind it, father. Don't be grieved."

Bob left the room and went upstairs to the room above, where Tiny Tim had died. There was a chair set close to the bed, and propped up against the chair, the little wooden crutch. Poor Bob sat down and when he felt a little composed he went back down again.

They sat before the fire and talked. Bob told them of the extraordinary kindness of Mr Scrooge's nephew whom he scarcely knew but who, on seeing Bob in the street that day, had come up to him and said how heartily sorry he was to hear of the death of Tiny Tim and how heartily sorry he was for Mrs Cratchit too.

"If I can be of service to you in any way," he said, giving me his card, "that's where I live."

"I'm sure he sounds a good soul!" said Mrs Cratchit.

"You would be certain of it, my dear," said

Bob, "if you saw and spoke to him. And I shouldn't be at all surprised if he got Peter a better job."

"Do you hear that, Peter?" said Mrs Cratchit.

"It's just as likely as not," said Bob. "But however and whenever we part from one another, I'm sure we shall none of us forget poor Tiny Tim — shall we — or this first parting that there was among us."

"Never, father!" they all cried.

"And I know that when we remember how patient and mild he was, we won't quarrel easily among ourselves and forget poor Tiny Tim in doing it."

"No, never, father!" they all cried again. "Then I am happy," said Bob, "very happy." Mrs Cratchit kissed her husband, his daughters kissed him, the two young Cratchits kissed him and Peter shook him by the hand.

"Spirit," said Scrooge, "something tells me that we will soon part. Tell me what man that was whom we saw lying dead."

The Ghost of Christmas Yet To Come conveyed Scrooge, as before, through narrow streets until they came to Scrooge's office.

Hastening to the window, Scrooge looked inside. Everything was the same as usual but the furniture was not his, and the figure sitting in the chair was not him. The Phantom pointed as he had done before.

On they went until they came to a neglected churchyard. It was walled in by houses, overrun by thick grass and weeds. The Spirit stood among the graves and pointed down to one. Scrooge advanced towards it, trembling.

"Before I draw nearer to that stone to which you point, answer me one question. Are these the shadows of the things that *will* be, or are they shadows of things that *may* be?"

Still the Ghost pointed downwards to the grave by which it stood.

"People can change," Scrooge went on. "And if they change, their ends must change too. Say that's the case with what you have shown me."

The Spirit was as unmovable as ever.

Scrooge crept towards it, trembling as he went. Following the line of the pointing finger, he read on the stone of the neglected grave: EBENEZER SCROOGE.

"Am *I* that man who lay upon the bed," he

cried in desperation.

The finger pointed from the grave to him, and back again.

"No, Spirit! No, no!"

The finger pointed still.

"Spirit!" cried Scrooge, clutching his robe even more tightly. "Hear me! I am not the man I was. I will not be the man I was. Why show me this, if I am past all hope?"

For the first time the hand of the Ghost appeared to shake.

"Good Spirit. I will honour Christmas in my heart and try to keep it all the year. I will live in the Past, Present and the Future. The spirits of all three will live within me and so will the lessons they have taught."

In his agony, Scrooge caught the Ghost's hand. It sought to free itself. Scrooge, desperate, held it tighter. But the Spirit, stronger, escaped. Holding up his hands in a last prayer to have his fate reversed, Scrooge saw a sudden change in the Phantom's hood and dress. It shrunk, collapsed, and dwindled down into a . . . bedpost.

5 The End of It

Yes! And the bedpost was his own! The bed was his own and the room was his own. But best and happiest of all, the time before him was his own, to make amends.

"I will live in the Past, the Present and the Future!" he repeated as he scrambled out of bed. "The Spirits of all three shall survive within me. Oh, Jacob Marley! Heaven and Christmas Time be praised for this. I say it on my knees!" He had been sobbing violently in his struggle with the Phantom and his face was wet with tears.

"They are not torn down," he cried, seeing the curtains round his bed. "They are here. *I* am here! I don't know what to do! I'm as light as a feather, as happy as an angel and as merry as a schoolboy! A Merry Christmas to everybody! A Happy New Year to all the world!"

He had rushed around the sitting-room so much that when he suddenly stopped he felt quite worn out.

"There's the door by which the Ghost of Jacob Marley entered!" cried Scrooge, dancing round the room again. "There's the corner where the Ghost of Christmas Present sat! It's all right, it's all true, it all happened. Ha, ha, ha!"

Really, for a man who had been out of practice for so many years, it was a splendid laugh, a most illustrious laugh. The father of a long, long line of brilliant laughs!

"I don't know what day of the month it is! I don't know how long I've been among the Spirits. I don't know anything. I'm quite a baby. Never mind. I don't care. I'd rather be a baby. Ha, ha, ha!"

Suddenly he stopped when he heard the church bells ringing out the lustiest peals he had ever heard. *Clash, clang, hammer, ding, dong!* Running to the window he opened it and put out his head. No fog, no mist; just clear, bright, jovial, stirring cold. Golden sunlight; heavenly sky; sweet fresh air; merry bells. Oh, glorious. Glorious!

"What's today?" he called out to a boy standing in the street below.

"Eh?" asked the boy, bewildered.

"What's today, my fine young fellow?" asked Scrooge again.

"Today!" replied the boy. "Today is Christmas Day!"

"It's Christmas Day!" said Scrooge to himself. "It's Christmas Day! I haven't missed it. The Spirits have done it all in one night. They can do anything they like. Of course they can! Of course they can. Hallo, my fine fellow!"

"Hallo!" replied the boy, again.

"Do you know the poultry shop in the next street, my fine young man?"

"I should hope I did."

"An intelligent boy! A remarkable boy! Do you know whether they've sold their prize turkey?"

"What, the one as big as me?"

"That's the one."

"It's hanging there now."

"Is it? Then go and buy it!"

"What?"

"Yes, yes," said Scrooge. "I mean it. Go and buy it and tell them to bring it here, so that I can give them the directions of where to take it. Come back with the man and I'll give you a shilling. Come back with him in less than five minutes and I'll give you half-a-crown."

The boy was off like a shot.

"I'll send it to Bob Cratchit, in Camden Town," whispered Scrooge, rubbing his hands and giving a splendid laugh. "He won't know who sent it. It's twice the size of Tiny Tim!"

Within a few moments the boy was back with the turkey and the man from the shop.

"— Here's the turkey!" cried Scrooge,

opening his front door. "Why, it's impossible to carry it to Camden Town. You must take a cab!"

The chuckle with which he said this, and the chuckle with which he paid for the turkey, and the chuckle with which he paid for the cab, and the chuckle with which he tipped the boy, were only to be exceeded by the chuckle with which he sat down breathless in his chair again, and chuckled till he cried.

Having shaved — which proved no easy task, for his hand continued to shake very much — and dressed in his very best clothes, Scrooge left the house. He looked so very pleasant and happy that people everywhere greeted him with a "How are you?" and "A Merry Christmas"!

He had not gone far when coming towards him he saw the two portly gentlemen who had walked into his counting-house the previous day, collecting money for the poor. It sent a pang through his heart when he thought what they must think on seeing him. But he knew what he

must do.

So going up to them, he said, "My dear sirs, "a Merry Christmas. I hope you were successful yesterday. It was very kind of you."

"Mr Scrooge?"

"Yes," said Scrooge. "That's my name, and I fear it may not be pleasant to you. Allow me to beg your pardon. And will you have the goodness of accepting . . ." Here he whispered in the first man's ear.

"Lord bless me!" cried the man. "Are you serious, sir?"

"Not a penny less, sir, I assure you! Call at my office tomorrow."

"We most certainly will!" cried the portly gentlemen. And it was clear that he meant it.

"Thank'ee," said Scrooge. "I'm much obliged to you. Bless you!"

He went to church and walked about the streets and watched the people hurrying to and fro, and patted children on the head and gave money to beggars. He had never dreamed that he could be so happy. Then, in the afternoon, he went to his nephew's house.

He passed the door a dozen times before he had the courage to go up and knock.

"Fred!" said Scrooge, when his nephew opened the door. "A Merry Christmas."

"Why bless my soul!" cried Fred. "Uncle Scrooge!"

"It's I. I've come to dinner. Will you let me in?"

Let him in! It's a wonder that Fred didn't shake his uncle's arm off. And when Scrooge had entered he felt at home within five minutes. Nothing could have been heartier. Wonderful party, wonderful games, wonderful happiness!

But early the next morning Scrooge was back in the office. If he could only be there first and catch Bob Cratchit coming late! That was the thing he had set his heart on.

And he did it! The clock struck nine. No Bob Cratchit. A quarter past. No Bob. He was eighteen minutes late! Scrooge sat with his door wide open so that he might see Bob come into the outer office.

Before he had even opened the front door, Bob Cratchit had taken off his hat and long, woollen scarf. Then, sitting down at his desk as quickly as he could, he began to write furiously,

trying to look as if he had been there all the time.

"Morning!" growled Scrooge, in a voice as normal as he could make it, when Bob finally entered. "What do you mean by coming here at this time of day?"

"I'm very sorry I'm late, sir," said Bob.

"Step this way, if you please."

"It's only once a year, sir. I won't do it again. I was making rather merry yesterday, sir."

"Were you, indeed. Now, I'll tell you what, my friend," said Scrooge. "I'm not going to stand this sort of thing any longer. And therefore I'm about — to raise your salary!"

Bob trembled. He thought Scrooge must have taken leave of his senses. Perhaps he should call for help and get him into a straight-jacket, quick!

"A Merry Christmas, Bob!" continued Scrooge. "A merrier Christmas, my good fellow, than I've given you for many a year! I'll raise your salary and help your struggling family. We'll talk it over this afternoon over a Christmas punch! Now, make up the fires and buy yourself a coal-scuttle before you do any work, do you hear?"

Scrooge was even better than his word. He did all that he said he would and much, much more. And to Tiny Tim, who did not die, Scrooge became a second father. He became as good a friend, as good a master and as good a man as the good old city knew — or any other good old city, in the good old world, for that matter. And if some people laughed to see him so much changed, he let them laugh and paid little heed.

He received no further visits from the Spirits. And it was always said of him that he knew, better than any man, how to celebrate Christmas. May that be truly said of all of us! And so, as Tiny Tim observed, *God bless us, everyone!*